T0380879

Michele
Jeanmarie

This is a work of fiction. All of the characters, names, incidents, organizations, and dialogue in this novel are either the products of the author's imagination or are used fictitiously.

Archway Publishing books may be ordered through booksellers or by contacting:

Archway Publishing
1663 Liberty Drive
Bloomington, IN 47403
www.archwaypublishing.com
844-669-3957

Interior Image Credit: Mary Sepúlveda

ISBN: 978-1-6657-6220-5 (sc)
ISBN: 978-1-6657-6221-2 (e)

Library of Congress Control Number: 2024913529

Print information available on the last page.

Archway Publishing rev. date: 07/03/2024

Stepping in the Shoe of Roy G Biv: A Soliloquy

Stepping in the Shoe of Roy G Biv: A Soliloquy

By
Michele Jeanmarie

The day would come when I would get my shoe, my favorite shoe. I had lost my shoe in the flood. Buckets of rain coursed through my city. Torrential waters pushed its way across houses, schools, businesses, barns, parks. It took everything in its way, living and nonliving, functional and nonfunctional, large and small. My shoes.

Rain had subsided, and we had come back to our home. We had lots of cleaning. Streetlights had been wacked, so had been street signs; trees had been snapped, so had been poles; cables had been cracked, except for the one which held my shoe. My shoe!

Settled in, most days I gazed through my window to catch a glimpse of my shoe: my shoe swaying and dancing clumsily across that one cable line. On windy days, I watched my shoe party to the rhythm of the winds. On rainy days, my shoe boogied to the pulse of the cable. On sunny days, my shoe tapped to the tempo of the clattering. My shoe!

One day, I gasped.

Where is my shoe? Shoe! I dashed out. It was no longer there. My shoe. It was no longer hanging on the cable line. I marched on, dizzily, I marched on. I swung around, and then again, but saw not my shoe. What I saw was a rainbow crowning my house. A bow arching across the clouds as a promise that not ever will water be sent out to destroy all mortal beings. Yet, there was this. I decided to find the beginning of the bow, the arc, the rainbow. I must find the beginning of the rainbow.

I ran and ran, glancing up occasionally. I ran some more, and some more. I was getting close to the end of the bow. I slowed down. I finally got there! There was a bucket. It was filled with shoes. My shoe!

I leaned in. Suddenly, I was sprinkled with gold, gold glitter. I fell back and saw my shoe. My shoe was ascending. Up, up and away my shoe ascended. My shoe!

My shoe is changing colors. Into the farthest arc of the rainbow, my shoe became **red.** Everything is red. There is much anger, much fury, much rage. Lots of groups are gathering together. Signs sport protests and solidarity, disillusionment and disgust. Red. My red shoe. My red shoe bolted out of there, only to collide into the orange arc.

What in your time might have occasioned such fury, such anger?
How was justice used to resolve it?

In **orange,** my shoe becomes orange! Here, there are priests and truth-sayers, teachers and students, historians and activists, artists and writers are communing to communicate ways to better tell the truths, full truths. Omission of truths *might* as well be lies. Disillusionment and disgusts. My shoe. My hopeful shoe. Is orange named after the color orange or is the color orange named after an orange!? My shoe scrams to yellow.

Was there ever a time you heard a partial truth and felt hurt, but when the full truth was revealed, you felt better?

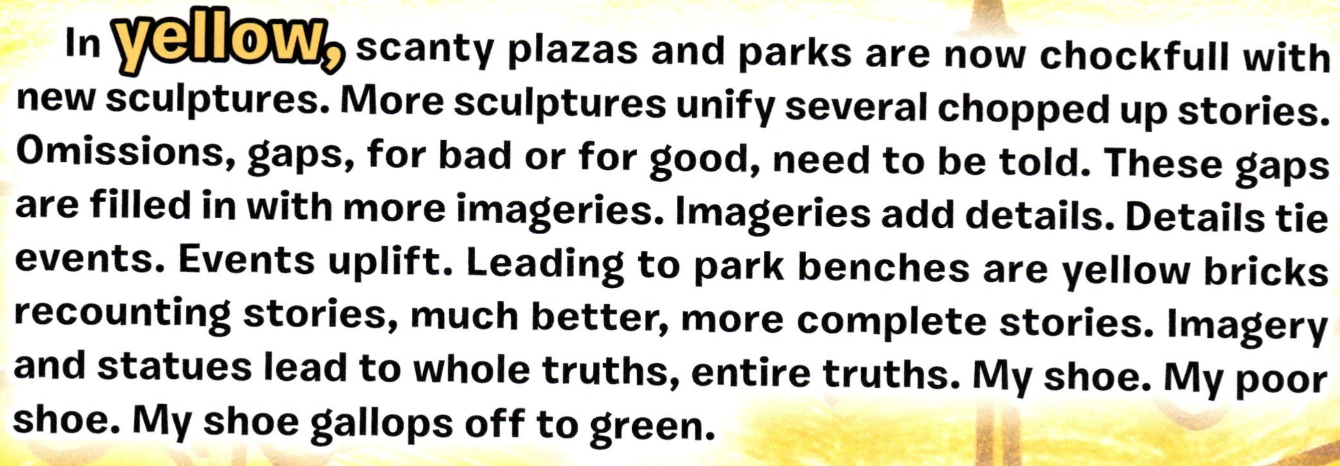

In **yellow,** scanty plazas and parks are now chockfull with new sculptures. More sculptures unify several chopped up stories. Omissions, gaps, for bad or for good, need to be told. These gaps are filled in with more imageries. Imageries add details. Details tie events. Events uplift. Leading to park benches are yellow bricks recounting stories, much better, more complete stories. Imagery and statues lead to whole truths, entire truths. My shoe. My poor shoe. My shoe gallops off to green.

Were you ever told a story only to later find out there was more to it? How did that make you feel? Has anyone ever said anything about you that was incomplete and made you feel poorly?

Green is envy. Opposite of envy is love, willing the good of the other. In green, engineers and architects revive burned down buildings. From hospitals to banks to ice cream parlors, from hair to nail salons, from upholstery shops to burger joints, many buildings are facing a new facelift, but why isn't there service for the poor? Why must they have to drive several zip codes away for a clinic, for healthcare? It's no wonder there is much envy, much green. My shoe. My shoe looks on. My shoe bounces to blue.

Were you ever saddened when someone received something, like a good grade, or a present that annoyed you?

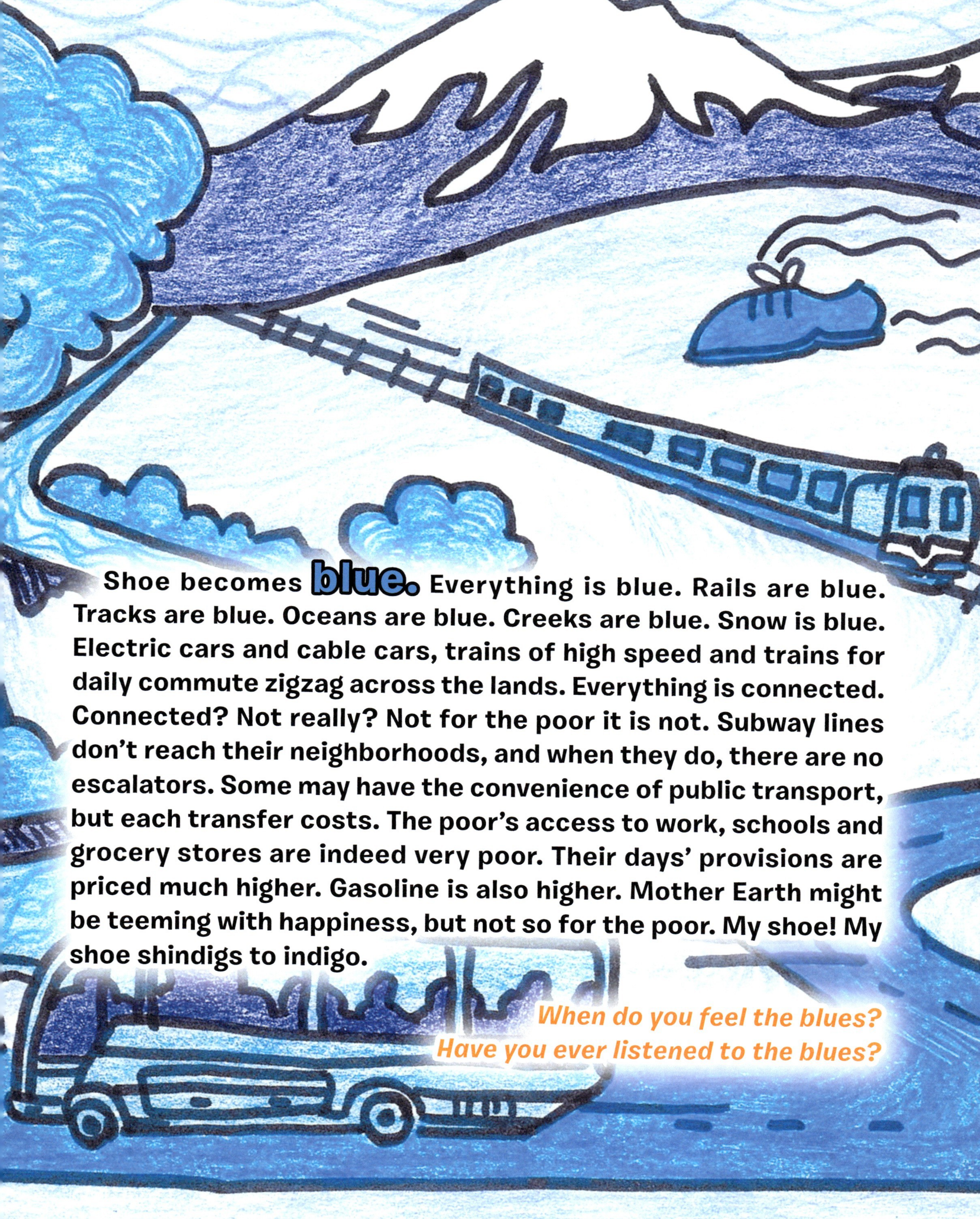

Shoe becomes **blue.** Everything is blue. Rails are blue. Tracks are blue. Oceans are blue. Creeks are blue. Snow is blue. Electric cars and cable cars, trains of high speed and trains for daily commute zigzag across the lands. Everything is connected. Connected? Not really? Not for the poor it is not. Subway lines don't reach their neighborhoods, and when they do, there are no escalators. Some may have the convenience of public transport, but each transfer costs. The poor's access to work, schools and grocery stores are indeed very poor. Their days' provisions are priced much higher. Gasoline is also higher. Mother Earth might be teeming with happiness, but not so for the poor. My shoe! My shoe shindigs to indigo.

When do you feel the blues?
Have you ever listened to the blues?

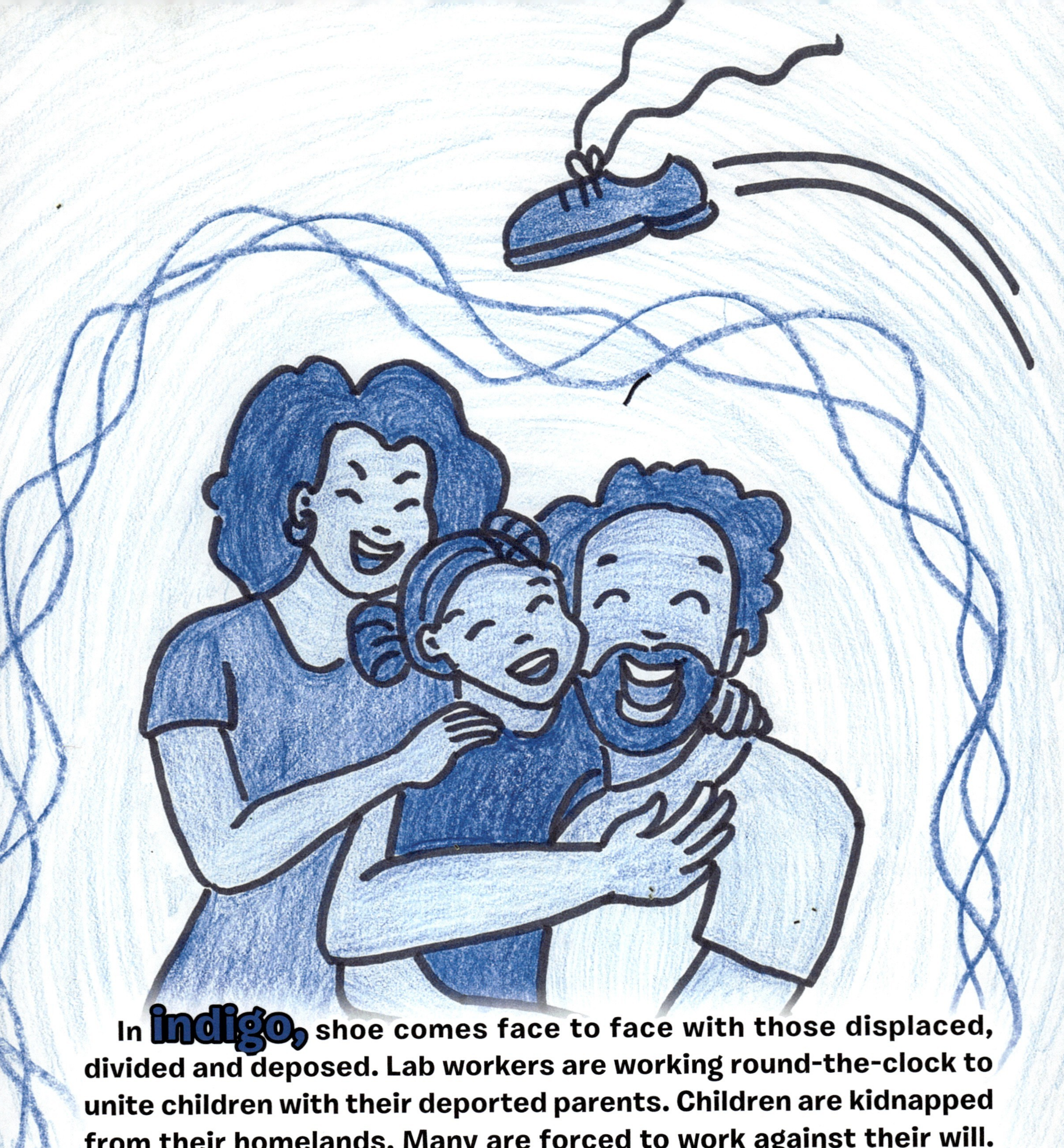

In **indigo,** shoe comes face to face with those displaced, divided and deposed. Lab workers are working round-the-clock to unite children with their deported parents. Children are kidnapped from their homelands. Many are forced to work against their will. Oh gosh, my shoe. My shoe. Can't take it anymore. My shoe! My shoe vaults to violet.

What causes violence and division?

My shoe is now **violet.** The Caribbean, the Amazon, and Africa are getting noticed. So are Latin America and the islands in the east. Solar panels, wind power, dams and hydroelectricity are dotting landscapes. But where? Dominant countries? Yep, when they could build co-partnerships to build infrastructure, to compensate for the thieving once done. Such cooperation will sure thwart illegal immigration. My shoe is feeling better. That's right, my shoe.

What else could be improved in your city to make shoe feel better?

Shoe! What is my shoe doing? BA! HA! HA! HA! My shoe, my shoe. My special shoe! I am almost there when my shoe POGOES back.

Back to violet, back to indigo, back to blue, back to green, back to yellow, back to orange, back to red. My shoe! My shoe! My shoe! My shoe POGOES back to the other end.

But where am I?

Hey, I am in my own backyard!

Activities Across the Disciplines

Also Known As:
Integrated Studies

It is known also as interdisciplinary studies.

It involves several topics and themes across disciplines to promote and engage student readers throughout the study.

It aims to target different learning styles offering multiple avenues to guide comprehension.

It is an effective approach in helping students become multifaceted learners while developing expertise in the discipline of choice.

It is a network of disciplines that enable students to develop meaningful understanding of complex associations.

It is coupled with project-based learning that makes school more interesting and productive for students and teachers alike.

Activities:

I. Science:

Define refraction.
Define light.
What is a rainbow?
How is it formed?

What are the colors of the rainbow? How many colors are there? Why did the author name her protagonist Roy G. Biv?
Why is red so much more vivid than the other colors?
Why is blue so weak?

Form a rainbow using a prism.

II. Language Arts:

A. Poetry:

Define soliloquy:
Explain how the author used it.
When someone says, “Let me get off my soapbox, what is implied?
Write your own soapbox.

B. Define anecdote:

How is an anecdote differed from a soliloquy?

The author wrote about several anecdotes. Called an anthology, a compilation of several stories, how did she tie them together?

C. In a diatribe, determine and summarize the conflict in each mini story. Was each conflict resolved, let's say, in another color of the rainbow?

D. Vocabulary:

Make a double entry dictionary of unknown words. Make a t-chart. On the left side, list all the unknown words. On the right side, write its synonym.

Use a vocabulary ladder to expand the meaning of each.

I. Civic:

What are your civic duties in your community, the global world and world economy? What are your social responsibilities, in other words? How does it contribute to the common good?

II. Career Day

Take-Your-Kid-to-Work-Day
Look and list all civic duties exhibited at your parent's job.
What are your parent's civic duties at his/her job?
What are their social responsibilities on and off work?
How do their social responsibilities help the common good?

III. Economics:

The author showed many people at work. List the jobs the author cited.
How does having a job, WORKING, support the dignity of the human spirit?
The goals of corporations are to make profit. How can they show their civic duty, still making a profit?
What are their civic duties, or responsibilities, toward the common good?
What can the government do to dignifying the human spirit?

IV. Art:

Value. Define it.
Monochromatic colors. Define it.
How does the author use color to add meaning to the context of each mini story?
Under civics, you stated the manner you would use your talent for the common good. Choose a color and illustrate how you would do this. Think of monochromatic colors needed to express it.

V. Theology:

A. What is Catholic Social Teaching?

a. List the seven principles

b. Summarize each one.

B. Research Dorothy Day and Catholic Workers Movement.

1. Are any of her efforts resonating today?
2. What might those be?
3. How can they be improved?
4. What can we do to improve upon them?

C. Explain this quote:

"What you do for the lesser one of you, you do to me."

D. Mother Teresa once said, "There is a lot of suffering, because we have forgotten that we belong to each other." Explain.